RESCUING THE DUPED BRIDE

MAIL ORDER BRIDES OF FIELDER'S UNION

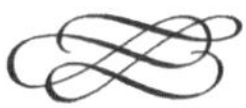

SUSANNAH CALLOWAY

Tica House Publishing

Sweet Romance that Delights and Enchants!

PERSONAL WORD FROM THE AUTHOR

Dearest Readers,

Thank you so much for choosing one of my books. I am proud to be a part of the team of writers at Tica House Publishing who work joyfully to bring you stories of hope, faith, courage, and love. Your kind words and loving readership are deeply appreciated.

I would like to personally invite you to sign up for updates and to become part of our **Exclusive Reader Club**—it's completely Free to join! We'd love to welcome you!

Much love,

Susannah Calloway

VISIT HERE to Join our Reader's Club and to Receive Tica House Updates!

https://wesrom.subscribemenow.com/

CONTENTS

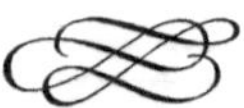

The dart sailed across the sheriff's office and embedded itself in the dart board with a solid thunk and a brief vibration. Danny Turner ventured over to it, leaned down to give it a squint, and then straightened back up with a smile.

"Whoo-ee. If it was any closer to the bull's eye, we'd have to get it a patch. You always have been a crack shot, Tom."

Thomas Barnett, thirty-one, lanky of form and laconic of personality, grinned at his friend.

"Must have been all those bandits I've taken aim at over the years. 'Course, never have been able to get any of them."

"Well, if they were nailed to the wall, I bet you would have."

Danny tossed the dart back onto Tom's desk and moseyed back to his own chair, leaning back far enough to prop it up against the wall behind him. Tom crossed one leg over the other and re-settled in his chair, tipping his head back to look at the wooden ceiling of the sheriff's office, which also happened to house the town's only jail cell. A jail cell, which was empty.

"Thanks for the words of encouragement, Danny. Times like these, a guy needs a friend like you as much as he needs a poke in the eye with a sharp stick."

"Aw, come on. You know I think you're the greatest sheriff that ever walked the earth."

Tom looked over at his deputy and raised one eyebrow.

"Can't help but suspect some sarcasm there."

"Well, you don't have to get all melancholy and take it out on me just because you can't figure out the Matrimonial Bandit."

Thomas Barnett groaned and rubbed his hands over his face. "For the last time, we are not calling him that."

"The Marriage Rogue," Danny suggested. "The Vow-Breaker. The Bridal Liar. The Mysteriously Disappearing Husband."

"Right," said Tom, sitting forward and reaching for the stack of papers on his desk. "I'm just gonna pretend you're not talking any more, got it?"

He busied himself with the stack. The good Lord knew he had plenty to do and little time to do it in. The last thing he should be doing was shooting the breeze with Danny – or listening to his deputy chuckling to himself over his own humor. But Tom couldn't help it. Danny Turner's words got to him, got under his skin. The fact was there had been five cases now, of unmarried women being called to Clayton County by a mysterious man who never seemed to appear. Each case almost identical to the others, and Tom was no closer to finding the answer than he had been over a year ago when it had all started.

First of all, it had happened in Smithville, two miles out of Fielder's Union. A young woman had arrived, insistent she had answered an advertisement in the Matrimonial Times, but the man she'd claimed to be writing to was unknown. His name had been Sullivan, Tom remembered. But there were no Sullivans in Smithville, which was a tiny town of only four hundred people. Impossible for someone to be unknown there; impossible for this Mr. Sullivan to hide. The girl had been flat broke after the journey to Arkansas from a town in West Virginia, and she had come to stay in Fielder's Union, unable to find a place to work in Smithville.

After that was Sybil Smith, *nee* Webb, the daughter of a wealthy man from Boston who had been looking desperately for a way out of her unhappy existence in the city. Well, she'd found it, even if it hadn't been what she'd planned. She had agreed to marry a man who had also written her a letter. This one was named Henry Miller, and he claimed to be a doctor in Fielder's Union.

Of course, the only doctor in Fielder's Union for the past forty years was old Doc Sanders, who was quite bemused when Thomas had tiredly asked him whether he'd ever had a younger colleague, student, or even an apprentice named Miller. At least Sybil Smith's story had turned out for the best after all.

The other three young women who had appeared over the past year and a half had not been so lucky. Gladys Bridgestone had been unable to return to New York. Ally MacIntyre had refused to be sent back to Mooretown, Connecticut, though she had never explained why. And Vila Brown had tried to make a go of it on her own, first finding work at the inn before she found that it simply wasn't enough to live on, and she had to find employment elsewhere.

All of them, bar Sybil Smith, had ended up in the local saloon, which had seen better days. Tom shook his head just to think of it. It had seen better owners, too. Marigold Henschel wasn't the kind of woman to shy away from hard work, but if she could get rich by having someone else do it, then she would.

Tom knew there was more to the saloon than a little too much drinking on the weekends – but it was a balance, a bargain he had to strike in order to keep peace in the town. Marigold kept her girls upstairs and ran a relatively clean establishment; Tom could find no quarrel with her methodologies, even if he despaired of her morals. But a good many of the upright men in Fielder's Union kept company with Marigold's upstairs girls, and it was too confusing a mix of politics for Tom to try and shut her down, as much as he wanted to.

Now, if he could somehow find out she had been behind the letters that had brought those unsuspecting girls here to Fielder's Union and pressured them into working for her, he could charge her with procurement…

But his instinct said he should look elsewhere.

He turned over a paper and sighed, rubbing at his forehead.

"Sometimes it just seems like I'm going around and around in circles," he said out loud.

"What else can you do?" asked Danny, who was picking at his nails as though he hadn't a care in the world. "Fielder's Union's only three streets wide."

Tom shot him a narrow-eyed glance, decided not to say anything, and reached for the next piece of a paper. This turned out to be an envelope, and he gave a low whistle as he fumbled in a desk drawer for a paper knife.

"What is it?"

"A letter."

Danny rolled his eyes.

"I figured that out, Tommy. Who are you getting letters from now? Don't tell me it's some girl. One of Marigold's girls, maybe."

Tom clenched his jaw but decided to let that jab pass. Danny knew full well how Tom felt about the subject.

"Not that it's any of your business, Deputy Turner, but it's from Melson."

Danny sat up straight. "Another letter from a US Marshal? You're coming up in the world."

Tom opened his mouth to reply to this, unable to hold back any longer from responding to his friend's jibes. But whatever he was about to say was lost to the noise of yelling that suddenly broke out down the street. Instantly, Tom was on his feet, patting swiftly at his side to ensure that his pistol was there and ready.

"Hold down the fort."

"You know I will."

Tom raced out of the sheriff's office, heading in the direction of the yells and calls. He'd been told once or twice he tended to overreact to things, but in his mind, it was always better to overreact than to fail to react enough. Fielder's Union was a relatively safe place to be, with a low crime rate. But low crime was not the same as no crime at all, and he prided himself on being a good sheriff.

However, now that he was outside in the cold wind of late January, it was easier to tell that the shouts were those of irritation rather than fright, anger, or distress. In fact, he could even figure out who was doing the shouting – that was the voice of Jimmy Logarty, he was certain.

Logarty was the owner of the mercantile. He was not known for his generosity and good humor, and his hoarse, rather throaty voice was often raised when demanding his clients make good on their credit. It was simply a bit louder today, and Tom wondered, as he slowed down his pace a little and headed for the store, who had failed to pay the merchant on time this month.

But it was his own name that he heard as he came up to the mercantile.

"Sheriff Barnett. Where is – aha, there you are, finally." Logarty spotted him and churned angrily toward him through the handful of spectators that always seemed to show up for any event, however minor, in Fielder's Union. Logarty was yanking a small boy along after him in his wake, and he pulled him all the way up to Tom as he stepped through the crowd, practically tossing the boy at the lawman. "Take him in. I mean it. That jail's been sitting empty long enough."

"Hold up, now," Tom said, lifting one hand to pacify Logarty and taking hold of the boy's shoulder with the other. "What's going on, Jimmy?"

"This little fiend has been stealing from me for weeks now. I finally caught him in the act – I knew someone had been doing it, but just wasn't sure who until I found him with his pockets full."

Logarty pointed a short, stubby finger at the child, who dropped his head and stared at the ground.

"And now I want him to pay it all back – or go to jail like the crook he is."

"Got it, Jimmy," said Tom. He turned the boy toward him. He couldn't have been more than ten or eleven, and he was a good two feet shorter than the tall, lanky sheriff. "Now, let's see here – you're Mary Guidone's oldest, aren't you?"

The boy nodded wordlessly.

"What's your name, son?"

"Oliver."

"Oliver Guidone, what will your ma say when she finds out you've been stealing from Mr. Logarty?"

This got the young boy's attention. His head flew up and he stared up at Tom with wide eyes.

"Oh, please don't tell her, Sheriff Barnett. She'll die of shame."

"And just about right, too," snorted Logarty loudly from the sidelines. Tom waved him into silence.

"How about you tell me why you did it, and I'll see whether I need to tell your ma – or if you should." He nudged Oliver's shoulder. "What did you take?"

"Beans," said Logarty.

Tom raised an eyebrow at the merchant. "Beans?"

Logarty nodded vigorously. "Three tin cans of beans."

Tom folded one arm across the other and chewed on his thumb for a moment, thinking this over.

"Well, Oliver," he said, "it seems to me beans are a mighty unlikely thing for a young man like yourself to steal on your own behalf. Tell me, how are things going at home?" The boy glanced up swiftly and just as swiftly down again. "Getting enough to eat?" No response. "How about your ma – and your little sisters?"

Still nothing. Tom sighed and patted Oliver on the shoulder.

"Folks," he said to the small crowd of onlookers who were still standing by in the hopes that something interesting would happen, "I'd be obliged if you'd go about your business."

He waited for a few moments as they dispersed, then turned his attention to Logarty. "Jimmy, would you do a favor for me? Hand those beans back over to Oliver and put them on my credit."

The merchant was stunned – and clearly incensed by the very notion.

"What – what…"

"You know I'm good for it. And I have a feeling Oliver here won't be stealing anything else. Will you, Oliver?"

Oliver shook his head, and Tom bent down to look him in the face.

"The Lord provides for good families," he said. "Your ma and your sisters and you – don't matter that your pa's gone, you four are still a family, and a good one, too. Next time there's a scarcity in your house, you go on and check in at the church. I reckon Mrs. Harlow will be mighty glad to have someone deserving to share the Lord's bounty with."

Oliver Guidone's eyes flew up to his, for just the briefest of flashes.

"Thank you, Sheriff," he whispered. Tom let go of his shoulder and the boy was off, running down the street. Tom shook his head.

"I can see why you couldn't catch up with him 'til now," he observed. "He's fast as a fox."

But Logarty was still fuming. "Sheriff, sometimes I think you're going soft on us."

"Aw, come on, Jimmy…"

"And sometimes I think," Logarty continued, "that your inability to figure out a simple mystery like them Mail Order Brides is taking away all your focus. That boy is a thief."

"He won't do it again."

"He's done it plenty of times already."

"His pa's only been gone for six months, Jimmy," Tom reminded him gently. "We must be kind to those in need."

Logarty shook his head. Muttering, "Soft, soft, soft," to himself, he went back into the mercantile and closed the door heavily behind him, flipping the sign over to read Closed.

Closed – it must be six o'clock, or thereabouts. The end of the day had come and gone without Tom really noticing, and the last of the pale daylight was dying on the wester horizon. He shivered; it was even chillier, too.

Arms wrapped about himself, he walked back down the street to the sheriff's station.

Danny looked up from his jigsaw puzzle. "Catch the crooks?"

"Of course, I did. I'm the sheriff." Tom rubbed at his jaw thoughtfully. "Danny, you don't think I'm getting soft, do you?"

His deputy snorted, stood up, and shoved him playfully by the shoulders to turn him back around to face the door.

"Tommy, you're tough as nails and twice as flat-headed. Now, I know your ma is making apple pie tonight because I smelled it from the window when I walked over this afternoon. Get home for supper or she'll make you wash the dishes."

"Right. Don't let the town burn down while you're on duty, Danny. You might lose some of your jigsaw pieces."

"See you tomorrow, Sheriff."

Tom walked home through the cold and the dark, wondering whether Logarty was right, wondering if he'd done the right thing by Oliver Guidone – and wondering how "a simple mystery" continued to elude the smart, dedicated sheriff of Fielder's Union.

CHAPTER 2

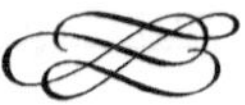

"Miss – Miss?"

It took the boy at the post office three tries before he was able to get Justine's attention, and she came back to reality only reluctantly, with a faint blush suffusing her pale cheeks as she realized there was now a line behind her, waiting for her to leave the counter.

"Oh, my goodness. I'm sorry, I was…"

"Distracted, I figured," chuckled the middle-aged woman who was next in line, nodding to the letter in Justine's hands. "I hope he's as good a man in reality as he is on paper."

Justine smiled her thanks for the woman's understanding.

"Oh, he is," she assured her fervently. "I just know it."

But as she left the post office, the faintest twinge of doubt crept in. Did she know it? She believed it with all her heart – but was it absolutely beyond question?

Just around the block, on one of the busiest streets in her neighborhood in Boston, she stopped to read over the letter again. With her fingertips she traced the neatly written address on the envelope – from Mr. Colin Williams of Fielder's Union, to Miss Justine Mayer of South Boston, Massachusetts. She heaved a romantic sigh. Even his penmanship seemed strong and upright.

And the letter itself –

She knew it was this letter, in particular, that had caused the reverie – and the doubt at the same time. She'd been expecting it. After all, they had begun their correspondence through his advertisement for a Mail Order Bride in the back of the Boston Globe. It was only through happenstance she had seen the advertisement – she was not a regular reader of the Globe, of course, especially given the fact that it had recently gone up to six cents a copy. She had enough trouble making ends meet at home, what with her sporadic employment and her father…

The thought brought on another sigh. Her father.

What would he say when she told him she was leaving?

She cringed at the thought. Boyd Mayer was not a cruel man by nature, but his words could be cutting, and he was not above giving his adult daughter his full opinion of anything she decided to do. Could she really leave him behind? After all, she was his only source of income – and all he had left.

But that very thought strengthened her resolve. Yes, she was his only source of income. And if she left him behind, perhaps he would be forced to stand on his own two feet for the first time since her mother had died, six years ago. Boyd Mayer was not an old man; his daughter was only twenty, and he was only forty-two. He had plenty of life and strength left in him to start anew, if he would only set his mind to it.

She knew, in her heart, that her guilty conscience, which had led her to provide her father with food, shelter, and spending money, was partly to blame for the predicament he was in currently. Oh, he had turned to drinking and gambling as soon as her mother had passed away. He'd been heartbroken. It had been up to Justine to go out and find work, piecemeal as it tended to be, simply so they could eat and have a roof over their heads.

But gradually, as she had gotten older and the money coming in had become steadier, he had begun to spend more and more time in the gambling halls. She wasn't even sure where he got most of his money to gamble with; she certainly couldn't give him enough to keep him out all day and half the night.

Realizing she was slipping into her usual routine of worrying over her father, she shook her head and began to walk once more. No, as difficult as it would be and as much as he might try to guilt and cajole her into changing her mind, she was determined. The letter from Colin she had received today contained his official proposal of marriage – and his urging to come west at once. She had set her hand to the plow, and she and her father would both fall to ruin if she turned back now.

Besides – she was in love with Colin. She was sure of it.

It was a strange thing to admit to herself. But it was the truth. In the two months they had been corresponding, she had found him to be a thoughtful, gentle man with an obviously strong work ethic, as well as a strong back. A silver miner. He had to be strong, to be carrying on such work and not shirking his duties even though he was approaching forty.

Nothing about Colin or the way she had found him was anything like the romantic ideal she had held for herself as a young girl. But now, at twenty years old and with only her drunken father for company, a simple life in Arkansas with a decent man sounded as romantic as a holiday in Europe.

All that aside, the idea of telling her father what her plans were still intimidated her. As she moved closer to home, she heard the distant whistle of a train and changed course suddenly, thinking swiftly over what she had in her pocketbook. Yes – yes, it should be enough to buy a ticket partway, and she could get another once she arrived at the end of that line, taking her all the way to Fielder's Union, Arkansas. That was, if there was a train all the way to Fielder's Union – she had a sneaking suspicion that at least part of the journey would have to be made by stagecoach.

Well, it would all be part of the adventure, she told herself, desperately aiming for cheerful positivity and trying to fend off the worry that rushed in on her each time she allowed her thoughts to stray back to her father. And with the courage of knowing there was a train ticket in her pocket, already bought and paid for, it would be that much easier to tell him of her decision – and stick to it.

With the precious ticket for the first leg of the journey tucked away safely in her pocketbook, she hurried home. The weak sunlight of late winter had peaked hours ago and was waning the moment she arrived back at the little flat she shared with her father. She wasn't expecting him to be in; he spent just about every evening out at the gambling hall or trying to cajole "old friends" to lend him more money to have a stake with. But when she pushed open the door, she knew at once he was home – and something was wrong.

There was a spot of something dark on the floor, just over the threshold. She pulled the door closed behind her and bent over it, curiosity warring with a warning voice in her mind. It was wet and a dark red.

Alarm rushing into her heart, she stood up straight swiftly.

"Dad?"

She heard something that might have been a soft groan from the other room. As quickly as she could with her fumbling fingers, she reached for the oil lamp that rested by the door and lit it to ward off the gloom. Then she carried it with her into the room, holding it high as though it could protect her from whatever she found.

Her father sat in his usual chair, slumped back, one arm wrapped over his middle. He shifted as she brought in the light, which reflected off the wide-blown pupils of his dark blue eyes – the only feature she had inherited from him.

"Jus…Justine…"

"Dad?" Nearly dropping the lamp in her haste, she rushed forward and got to her knees beside him. He was in a terrible state; she saw the blood seeping over his fingers, his protecting hand, and her heart clenched within her. "Dad, can you speak? What happened?"

"Old…friends…"

Justine felt the spark of anger and terror and a huge, unscalable sorrow. She knew what he meant without him having to say it. He had been in debt up to his eyeteeth, more than likely. Well, she'd never had the money to pay off what he had lost, and he had long since left off asking her for more than dribs and drabs. He must have gambled harder to try to make up for the riches he had lost – and made a bad bet.

The last bad bet he would ever make, she was afraid.

The wound was deep, and she put his hand back over it, pressing on his palm though she knew there was nothing that would stop the bleeding.

"Hold still, Dad – everything's going to be just fine. Stay here and don't move, I'll run for the doctor."

She started up but with a startling swiftness his other hand had closed over hers.

He shook his head and looked into her eyes.

"No time left," he said in a hoarse whisper. "I'm…sorry, Justine…"

"Oh, Dad." Tears welled up in her eyes, but she fought to keep them at bay. She must not let him see she was about to cry – not in his final moments. She couldn't let him slip into his eternal rest thinking he had brought her nothing but sorrow. With an effort, she managed a tremulous smile, lifting her hand to cup his cheek. "Don't worry about it now. You did your best to raise me right."

"Only good thing I ever did…'cept for marryin' your mother…Justine…I should have left something for you…"

She shook her head, firming her lips to stall another round of threatening tears.

"No, Dad. I'll be all right. I'm – I'm going west to Arkansas. A man out there wants to marry me. He'll take care of me, Dad, don't you worry…I'll be just fine."

"Not a…gambler…is he?"

A faint spark of humor was in his eyes, the faintest twist of a smile on his lips.

"No, Dad, he's a miner – he works in a silver mine."

"Ah…good. Dress my daughter in…the finest silver…" The rest of his words were lost in a nearly noiseless murmur as he drifted closer and closer to his eternal rest. The blood had slowed, but she knew there was no chance of recovery from a wound this grievous. She wondered if he would tell her who had done this to him. But she knew he would not. In her father's mind, after all the years he'd spent gambling and borrowing and never paying back, the man who had killed him was probably well within his rights.

She knew it without understanding it; how her father could have let himself get to this state was beyond her. But it must have been desperation – and she knew a little bit about desperation.

She felt desperation now, as she saw her father's eyes close for the last time, watched his final half-breath before everything stopped.

For a long time, Justine sat there with her head buried in her father's shoulder, while the world outside darkened, and she finally stopped fighting against the tears.

CHAPTER 3

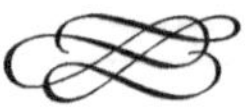

In the second week of February, on a Tuesday afternoon that was far too quiet for his taste, Thomas Barnett was grateful to see his little sister Faith step into the sheriff's office. He sat up at once, a grin sweeping over his narrow face.

"Boy, am I glad to see you."

"Glad to see me?" Faith asked, smiling back at him and hoisting the picnic basket she held on her arm. "Or glad to see this?"

"Guess that depends on what's in it."

She raised an eyebrow at him, and he laughed.

"I'm just teasing you, Faith. You know you're the light of my life."

"Yes, well, I also know how you feel about Ma's apple pie, so perhaps you'd better just take this basket before you tell any more little white lies."

She handed it over to him, and he got up and took it gladly, reaching out to rumple her brunette braids. His sister was only nineteen, more than a decade younger than he was, and one of the sweetest people he'd ever met – especially to other people, who happened not to be her older brother.

"What's Ma up to, anyhow? She didn't send you packing over here with the basket just because she didn't feel like an outing, did she?"

Faith chuckled. "You know her better than that – she's at the mercantile, of course, having a chat with Mr. Logarty."

"Poor Ma," said Thomas, with heartfelt sincerity. Faith waved the comment away.

"The dance is coming up in a few weeks, and she wants to make sure there will be plenty of supplies for all the baking that the Ladies' Committee is planning on. Georgiana Frost is *determined* we won't run out of pies this time."

"Well, she'd better not let me in the door, then," Tom said, opening the basket and taking out the paper-wrapped parcel that held a wide slice of his mother's apple pie. Eliza Barnett was the best baker in Fielder's Union, if not the county as a whole, and he'd fight to the death anyone who dared to say otherwise, or bring them in to cool their heels in the jail cell for a while, at the very least. "Why didn't you go with her to the meeting? You're a lady too, aren't you?"

Faith shrugged as though the idea hadn't really occurred to her and meandered over to the chair that sat against the wall. "I figured you'd need something to cheer you up. After all, there hasn't been a ruckus in town in weeks."

Tom grinned over at her, then took his first bite of pie.

"That's true. Not since Oliver Guidone. I'm beginning to wonder whether something's gone terribly right."

"Well," said Faith, getting around to her point gradually, so as not to scare him off, "since things are going so well – what do you say to showing your face at the dance this year?"

Tom sat back, toying with his fork.

"I should have figured you'd have an ulterior motive in coming here."

"Aw, come on, Tom," Faith wheedled. "There's no reason why you shouldn't…you went last year."

"That's right, I did – and that's why I didn't want to go again. It's just a reminder, Faith…" He stopped and swallowed hard, thinking over what might be the right words to say. How could he tell his little sister that the dances and other social events that the Ladies' Committee so dearly loved to put on only served to make him think of how alone he was?

He could get along without thinking about it, most of the time. But when it came to a dance, with the whole town there, it was impossible to attend without realizing that there were very few women around these parts, and what seemed like far too many men. The women that were there were drawn to the younger men, not the ones who had reached their thirties without being married and who espoused a dedication to the law that overruled any potential affection for a woman.

He rubbed the back of his neck. Of course, part of that was just him trying to protect himself, he knew. He was uncomfortably aware of the fact that it would be far too easy to sink into a despair if he thought too long and hard on the likelihood that he would ever start a family of his own.

And what was worse, almost, was the knowledge that a few of the potentially marriageable girls were upstairs above the saloon, having chosen the quicker path to being taken care of. The waste of it, the shame, would eat away at him if he let it.

Well, the most he could do there was be determined not to let it happen anymore. And find out who was writing those phony letters…

"Tom?"

His sister's voice was gentle. She was sitting forward on her seat, smiling at him winsomely, her hands gripping the edge of the chair waiting for his response.

He sighed and leaned forward, smiling at her.

"I'll think about it, Faith. I promise."

Her face fell a little, but she rallied – she really was a positive person, he thought. A real go-getter, too. He couldn't have been prouder of her if she was his own daughter.

"All right," she said, standing up. "I'll leave you to your pie, then – and remind you there's plenty more where that came from…if you decide to go to the dance."

She turned toward the door but was stopped in the midst of her exit by the entrance of Deputy Daniel Turner, accompanied by a young woman.

Tom had looked down at his paperwork again with a studied busyness, though he was in reality looking sadly at the last few bites of his pie. It wasn't until Danny cleared his throat meaningfully that he looked up – and his heart stuttered to a brief stop.

Almost immediately, it picked up again, beating far more quickly than was its wont.

The lady with him was – well, it was hard to put his finger on it exactly. She was fair-haired, blue-eyed – but he'd seen blue-eyed blondes before. There was something different about this one. Perhaps it was the surety with which she stood, as though she had set her mind to something and was not about to let anything stand in her way. Or perhaps it was the tracks of tears down her cheeks, nearly imperceptible but there. Or perhaps it was the particular color of her eyes, the darkest blue he'd ever seen, the color of the lake outside town on a calm, still winter's morning.

Without realizing it, he was standing up at his desk.

"Got another one for you, Tommy," said Danny, and held his hand out to the young woman, inviting her to step forward toward Tom's desk. "He's the sheriff, ma'am. I'm sure he'll know just what to do."

"Another one?" Tom asked, feeling bewildered – and not liking it one bit. He usually felt calm and self-assured when at the sheriff's station. Living a life of potential danger was his chosen environment. How was it possible that the entrance of one young woman he didn't know could throw him off his stride so badly? If she would just stop looking at him like that, he would have a chance to recover…

But she didn't stop looking at him. She took a seat across from the desk, and he sank back into his own chair, and their eyes did not break their union for a single second along the way.

In the background, Faith closed the door without leaving and stepped back toward them, softly.

"That's right," said Danny, going to his own desk and taking a seat. "I came across her at the stage stop. She'd been waiting for over an hour."

"Oh, poor thing." said Faith, rushing to the fireplace and putting the kettle on. "You must be freezing."

"Waiting for what?" Tom asked, still unable to look away from the unknown woman. Finally, her lips moved, and she spoke.

"Who," she corrected him softly. "I was waiting for Mr. Colin Williams. He works here at the Fountain Silver Mine, just outside of Fielder's Union. He is thirty-nine years old, just under six feet tall, and has black hair and a mustache. I am engaged to be married to him."

Tom's heart sank. Bad enough to think this extraordinary creature was already claimed by someone else – and worse still that he was about to have to break the news to her.

He leaned forward, taking a deep breath to steel his nerves.

"There is no Fountain Silver Mine here in Fielder's Union," he said. "Far as I know, there's no silver mine in Clayton County. We don't have much that's worthwhile, here in this part of Arkansas… and the name of Mr. Colin Williams doesn't ring a bell, either." He hesitated. "I'm sorry to have to tell you that, miss."

For a moment, he thought she wasn't going to respond at all. Her eyes flickered rapidly, lashes fluttering, and then she got ahold of herself.

"Yes – I have been told. I had supposed the deputy just might not have known…but he assured me that you've lived here since you were a child and knew everyone and everything."

"Well, that's going a little far," Tom said, resisting the urge to glare in Danny's direction. "For instance, I don't know you."

"I'm not from here."

"Where are you from?"

She paused briefly, and he saw a flare of sadness in her eyes. Regret over something she had lost, perhaps, something she had left behind.

"Boston," she said.

Tom let out a sigh and sat back in his chair, rubbing his hand over his forehead.

"You're right," he said to Danny. "She's another one."

"I don't know why you two keep saying that," said the woman, frowning at him. "Could you explain it to me?"

"I'm sorry to have to, but I guess I should." Tom leaned forward again, steepling his hands in front of him on the desk. "The way of it is, Miss – may I ask your name?"

"Mayer. Miss Justine Mayer."

"Miss Mayer." He pressed a hand to his chest. "Sheriff Thomas Barnett – but please call me Tom. Miss Mayer, the truth of it is that there's been a problem for the last year or so round about Fielder's Union." He quickly explained the mystery of the Mail Order Brides, keeping it as short as possible and avoiding too many details, as she was looking more and more upset as he went on. By the time he had finished, she had one hand covering her mouth. Above it, her blue eyes were bright with unshed tears.

"Here, dear," Faith whispered to her, handing her a cup of tea. "Drink this – you'll feel better. Warmer, anyhow."

She dragged a chair over from the wall and sat down next to Miss Mayer, patting her hand.

"Well, that's the long and the short of it," Tom finished up, glancing briefly at Danny, who nodded at him and resumed picking at his nails. "I'm awfully sorry about it, too."

"He really is," Faith assured her. "He's been a wreck about it, with all the other girls."

Tear-widened blue eyes looked up at Tom.

"What happened to them?" she asked.

Tom scratched at the back of his neck, wondering if there was any way to get out of answering. His sister, with a do-good attitude that was typical of her, leapt into the gap.

"They're here in town," she said. "But the most important thing is that you have somewhere to stay while we sort things out – and you can stay with us." She glanced swiftly at her brother. "Can't she, Tom?"

Tom hesitated – a bit too long. The girl's eyes flooded with tears once more, this time threatening to spill over completely, and Faith glared at him.

"Of course," he answered, hastily. "Of course, she can. Ma will be delighted. We've got the spare room, and there's always plenty to eat at the supper table." He managed a weak smile. "And I'll get it sorted out, believe you me. You're the last girl this is going to happen to, Miss Mayer."

Her eyes, despite the tears, were fixed on his once more. She wanted to believe him, he sensed – and he wanted to believe his own words just as much. He was painfully aware that he had promised just such a thing before…and failed.

Well, this time would be different, he vowed. He would make good on that promise.

And if Miss Mayer with the wide blue eyes was to live under his roof for any length of time, he was mightily afraid that he would find himself making other promises, too.

CHAPTER 4

In the third week of February, with the distant promise of spring growing closer by the day, Justine Mayer woke up from an unsettling dream with the sense that someone had called her name.

For a long moment, she lay absolutely still and listened, every fiber of her being concentrating on catching and dissecting every little sound. But there was nothing apart from the faint hum of the town outside the window as Fielder's Union began to wake up and go about its business. And now, as she listened, she could hear the sound of dishes and pots and pans rattling downstairs as Eliza Barnett began to get breakfast together for her little family, which had so recently and unexpectedly grown by one lost Bostonian.

The sound was comforting – just as comforting as the thought of Eliza herself. Justine smiled to herself, content to lay there for a few moments and listen, letting the everyday sounds of the happy, comfortable existence among the Barnett family drown out the echoes of her dreams.

She had been there in Fielder's Union for a week now, and still she wasn't sure what the future held. She was grateful, though, for how welcoming her new friends had been; Faith Barnett was an absolute delight, kind and gentle but with an unwavering loyalty to those to whom she became attached, as she had evidently become attached to Justine. And her mother Eliza was the most motherly person Justine had ever met. She could not help but think back to years before, when she was still a child, and how her own mother had been. In the six years since her mother had fallen asleep in death, Justine had never been made to feel so welcome, so wanted, and so loved.

And they had only known her a week. She stepped onto their veranda a complete stranger and walked into their house an old friend.

There was no doubt of the fact that the warmth and friendliness of the Barnett family was what helped Justine to cope with the difficulties that stretched out in front of her without an obvious end. Yes, Sheriff Barnett had promised he would get to the bottom of who was writing the false letters to bring Mail Order Brides from Boston to Fielder's Union. But even should he do so, what then? She was faced with the choice of going back to Boston – the very thought of which filled her with a frantic feeling of panic – or finding employment or another living situation here in Fielder's Union…or going somewhere else.

As intimidating as the first two options were, they were nothing compared to the last choice. Here, at least, she had Faith and Eliza…

And the promised protection of the town's handsome young sheriff.

At this particular thought, Justine decided she'd had just about enough of lying around in bed. Chastising herself for her wayward thoughts of the sheriff, she got out of bed and went to wash her face and comb her hair at the basin in the corner. If it was the only wayward thought, perhaps it wouldn't have been such a problem. The trouble was, however, that in the week since she had been there in Fielder's Union – in fact, almost from the moment she set foot in the sheriff's office. – her thoughts had become wayward more and more frequently…

It would help, she told herself as she changed into her dress and headed for the stairs, if he wasn't so very handsome. And if he wasn't so heroic in his determination to help her out. So dedicated to his profession. It wasn't just that the last thing she needed was to become attached to another man, even if the first one turned out not to have existed to begin with. It was that she had a sinking feeling she was already becoming attached – and yet Thomas Barnett was the most dedicated, determined, hard-working man she'd ever met.

In her heart, she was positive she would never be able to compete for his attention when her chief competitor was the pursuit of justice. Sheriff Barnett was just too – just too dedicated, too honest, and upright and good.

In fact, he was a whole host of things that made it ever harder to listen to her own better judgement and avoid setting her heart on him. Yes, it was a distraction from her puzzling and distressing predicament, but at what cost would the distraction come?

She was still shaking her head at herself when she entered the kitchen. Eliza Barnett, a cheerful woman with steel-gray hair and a motherly demeanor who was nearing sixty in years but only thirty in outlook, greeted her with a smile and a teasing comment.

"What, haven't even had breakfast yet and already someone's said something you disagree with? Perhaps you'd better save your conversations until after you've had some coffee."

Justine smiled back and took a seat at the table, where the thoughtful older woman had already set out three clean mugs ranged around the coffee pot.

"If I could avoid conversations with myself, I certainly would."

"Ah, arguing with yourself at this time of day? It's a difficult thing, for sure." Eliza shook her head and chuckled. "What was the argument about, if I may ask? And who won?"

Justine hesitated – but of course she could not bring herself to tell the entire truth about just what she'd been thinking of. Instead, she side-stepped.

"About my future," she said. "About the prospect of returning to Boston – I had a dream that made me think of it, I think."

"Is that so?" Eliza sat down beside her with eyes filled with concern. "You know you needn't make any decisions now, especially before Tom figures out who wrote those letters. You're welcome to stay here with us as long as you like. No need to rush into anything."

"I know, and I appreciate it." She hesitated, biting her lip. "I dreamed – about my father, I think. He was calling to me, calling my name."

"Your words make it sound as though it could have been a nice dream, but your face says otherwise," Eliza observed quietly.

"Yes." Justine was quiet for a moment. She had told the Barnetts, briefly, that she had no living family and that her father had died just recently. But she hadn't yet told them how recently, or the violent and tragic circumstances of his death. She wasn't sure why, other than she yearned for them to see her as herself, not as a victim of what had happened to her family. And in her heart, she supposed, she was ashamed of what her father had done that had caused him to lose his life. What if the Barnetts saw her as simply a product of the father who had raised her, tainted by a family history of gambling and drinking?

In her heart, she knew they would think no such thing. But there was always the chance she was wrong – she'd learned the hard way, with Colin, that she tended to trust too much, too quickly.

"He died only a month ago," she ventured at last. "And – quite suddenly." She dropped her eyes to the table. "I was with him – I was the only one with him."

"Poor dear," Eliza murmured, reaching out to put a hand over Justine's. "No matter what or how it happens, it's always a tragedy to lose someone we love. And then to put all your eggs in one basket and come here expecting to marry – well, you've had far more sadness than your due."

"Perhaps it's just bad luck," Justine said quietly.

But Eliza shook her head.

"Whether it is or it isn't remains to be seen," she said. "Scripture says that time and chance happeneth to us all. But for every bad thing that happens, there's sure to be something good happening along right behind. Something tells me you've got more than one good thing waiting in the wings, my dear, to make up for all the bad."

She squeezed Justine's hand and stood up from the table. "Now, I've got a meeting with the Ladies' Committee this afternoon. Would you like to come along with me? It'll be just the thing to take your mind off your troubles, for goodness knows we've got more troubles among the Committee than anyone. Sometimes we ladies can't agree on anything."

Justine couldn't help but laugh at the frank admission.

"If there's anything I can help with, I'd be glad of the distraction."

"I'm sure we'll find something. Georgiana always has a new plan up her sleeve, and it'll take someone younger than me to keep up with her. We've got the dance coming up, you know, and it's not just a matter of food, but what about drink? Cordial is all right in moderation, but at the harvest dance, my dear, you wouldn't believe it, three young men tried to spike the punch independently of each other, and you can imagine the effect…"

She continued on, more and more involved in her story by the moment, and Justine was content to sit and listen. Any moment, she knew, Faith and Sheriff Barnett would come down for breakfast, and they would sit around the table in the warm kitchen and chat and laugh. The day would seem brighter, the future seem more clear, and she would look forward to the afternoon with the Committee. She spoke the truth when she told Eliza she would be grateful for the distraction – not just from her past, or her future, either.

Anything that could distract her from her unceasing inner vision of the dedicated young sheriff would be heartily welcomed.

CHAPTER 5

Thomas Barnett was not a timid man, and rarely did he shrink away from speaking exactly what was on his mind. At the muttered string of mild curses that escaped his lips that morning, his deputy looked up from his desk with amusement.

"Well, gee whillickers, Tommy. Tell me how you really feel."

Tom dropped a fat stack of papers back on his desk with a loud thump and sat back in his chair, rubbing his hands over his face.

"What on earth happened to that letter, is what I want to know."

"What letter?" Danny returned to his own work, apparently not caring much what the answer was.

"The letter from Adrian Melson."

"Hmm?"

Tom narrowed his eyes at his deputy. "You're never going to get anywhere if you don't pay attention to things like this, Danny."

Danny raised his head at this, fire flashing in his eyes. "So you say, but I'm not the one who oh so carelessly misplaced a letter from a US Marshal," he retorted sharply. In the next second, though, his mood switched abruptly, and he continued on placidly. "Maybe it went out with the trash by accident. Or got burned up when we made the fire this morning."

"I guess it could be." Tom rubbed his forehead. "It's my own fault for forgetting about it until now. It's been a whole week, after all. Guess I was distracted."

"Guess you were," said Danny, leaning back in his chair and giving him a grin that positively leered. "I would be, too, if I had a pretty young female addition to the household."

Again, Tom narrowed his eyes at the other man, though with less good humor this time.

"I don't want to hear you bandying things about."

"Who's bandying? I'm just voicing my own opinion."

"Well, kindly avoid forming opinions about Miss Mayer. The poor thing has enough troubles without you adding grist to the rumor mill."

"Who's adding grist? I just stated a fact. She is living with you, isn't she?"

And he was right about that. Justine Mayer had come home with Faith a week ago, and there she had stayed. She was across from him at every mealtime, said a sweet goodnight to him when she went to bed of an evening, helped out his ma with the cooking and cleaning, and was good company for his little sister. And if she was distractingly pretty, and occupied his thoughts rather more than he wanted, well, that was nobody's business but his own. Besides, the main thing was tracking down the culprit behind the false letters; it only made sense that she would stay around Fielder's Union until the job was completed.

If she chose to move on afterward, he wouldn't try to stop her.

He might want to, but he wouldn't.

None of this addressed the comments Danny had made. Nor did they address the arched eyebrows with which he was waiting for a response.

"Yes, she is," Tom said at last, but added quickly, "but only to avoid needing to go to work at the saloon. Too many of the girls who have fallen victim to the false letters have ended up there as it is. I won't let her be another."

"You're quite passionate about it."

"It's a matter of justice. Of course, I'm passionate about it."

"Oh, and it's justice that raises your passion, is it?"

Another sly comment, another arched eyebrow. Tom gritted his teeth and turned away from his deputy.

"Danny, it's just as well we're friends, because if we weren't, I don't think I'd like you much, sometimes."

"No? That's too bad, boss, because I think you're just dandy."

But even that was a jibe, and Tom had a sneaking suspicion his own feelings were mutually reciprocated in the same manner. Danny wasn't a bad man, or a bad deputy, though he did tend to only pay attention to things that personally interested him. But he was unpredictable. It was impossible to know from one moment to the next whether he was being entirely sincere.

They had lived in the same town and worked in the same sheriff's office for years, and Tom wasn't sure he was any closer to really knowing Danny now than he had been when they'd first met.

"I reckon I'd better write Marshal Melson another letter and explain that I misplaced his first one."

"Don't forget to explain that you never bothered to read the first one even when you were holding it in your hands," Danny suggested.

"You know it was because of what happened with Oliver Guidone that I didn't – and then next thing I know you're bringing in Miss Mayer…'"

"And anyone would be distracted by Miss Mayer, sure, sure," said Danny, standing up and stretching. "Look, I'm sorry, Tommy, I'm just teasing you. You know how I am."

"I guess," said Tom, somewhat grumpily.

"Say, how about I go down to the café and rustle us up some grub? That way neither of us have to take the time to go home, and we can stay focused on the case."

"Well – I guess that would be all right."

"If you finish that letter off to Marshal Melson, I'll drop in at the post office and make sure it gets sent off today. How about that?"

Sometimes, Tom thought, Danny must realize how obnoxious he could be and decide to make up for it by going out of his way to be as sweet as pie. It was a little unnerving, if he was being honest with himself.

But still, it was obvious that his deputy was extending the hand of friendship with his offer, and it would be crass to turn him down.

"All right," he said, reaching for a blank sheet of paper. "Give me just a minute."

"Sure."

Tom dashed off a note to Marshal Melson explaining that his previous letter had been lost, unopened and unread, and asking for a repeat of the information. After a moment's thought while he chewed on the end of his pen, he added another paragraph.

I regret to say that there has been yet another victim of the mysterious false letter writer. Miss Justine Mayer, late of Boston, Massachusetts, arrived in Fielder's Union last week expecting to meet a Mr. Colin Williams who, of course, does not exist. I continue with my investigative efforts but have yet to take any steps closer to finding out who has sent these letters and so badly misled these innocent women. Should you come across any more information regarding the culprit, I'd be pleased to accept your help as often as you can offer it.

He signed it quickly, folded it into an envelope that was already addressed with Marshal Melson's current station, and handed it over to Danny, who was putting on his coat. Danny slipped the envelope into his pocket and patted it, giving Tom a wink.

"Well, no worries, it's safe with me. I'll be back in a jiffy, Tommy."

Tom waved him away as he left, letting in a cold blast of air from the street outside. The air contended briefly with the warmth from the fireplace, and Tom got up to put another log in the stove to help it out. For a moment, he sat crouched before the open fireplace door, holding the poker and lost in a reverie as he watched the flames.

Someday, he thought, he would be sitting here about to go home, and there would be a loving wife waiting for him. He wouldn't feel so alone, so separated from men his own age. He wouldn't be so dependent on his mother and sister for companionship.

And he would have settled the question of the mysterious letter writer once and for all.

He set the poker down and went back to his desk with a sigh.

"Sometimes, Thomas Barnett," he told himself out loud, "it's hard to tell whether you're coming or going. What are you most concerned about – justice and truth and lawful peace, or your own sorry self?"

Why did it seem so much more difficult, all of a sudden, to keep his mind on his work? Sure, Faith had asked him about going to the dance, but she had pestered him about the last one, too. There was no earthly reason why he should keep finding himself drifting into a daydream about dancing at the upcoming event, with a certain Miss Justine Mayer wrapped in his arms…

Things would be easier, he told himself, if she hadn't come to stay with them. But then again, if she hadn't come to stay with them, she might even now be forced to seek work at the saloon. And he couldn't stomach the thought of someone like her falling so low.

It was just as well that Danny had offered to bring in food for the noon meal. He shrank from the idea of going home to sit down to dinner with Justine – the thought gave him butterflies in the stomach. Uncomfortable butterflies, too.

At the same time, he found himself craving her company, the sight of her, the sound of her voice.

He wrestled with himself all through the rest of the afternoon, alternately redoubling his determination to stay focused on his work and accidentally slipping back into the daydream. By the time the sunlight began to fade from the sky, he was exhausted – and still had plenty more to do.

"Night, boss," Danny said, waving as he headed for the door.

"Sure," Tom said absently, turning over the page he was looking at. His deputy paused at the door.

"You are going to go home, aren't you, Tom? I mean – you're not going to sleep here at your desk again."

Tom glanced up at him. "Aw, come on, I haven't done that for months."

"Sure, but I'll never forget the shock it gave me, coming in here one morning and finding you passed out with your head on the table," Danny said, grinning. "I'd have thought you had a heart attack and died if you hadn't started snoring."

"I'm the sheriff of Clayton County, Danny. I have to take my work seriously."

"Sure," Danny called over his shoulder as he left. "But that's not what they mean when they say to sleep on it."

Despite his deputy's teasing words, Tom turned his attention back to the task at hand and continued on. The next time he looked up from the pages in front of him, he had completed a significant portion of the backlog against which he'd been struggling ever since the beginning of the mysterious letters, and it was completely dark outside. He glanced at his pocket watch and muttered a curse to himself. He'd worked straight through supper – it was nine o'clock.

Abandoning the rest of the papers on his desk, he wrapped his coat around himself and hurried home through the late winter darkness.

As he had feared, his house was nearly completely dark, with only an oil lamp burning in the window of the kitchen. He closed the front door behind him as quietly as possible; the house was silent.

But the silence was misleading. When he entered the kitchen, it was to find Justine Mayer seated at the table, a cup of tea before her and her head bent over some mending. The oil lamp was pulled close to her, and her blonde hair shone in the light. There was a breathtaking quality about the scene, as though it were a fine painting by one of the old masters.

"Oh." He stopped in the doorway, and she looked up. Her blue eyes went directly to his, and she smiled gently.

"Come in, come in."

"I didn't realize how late it was getting," he said, feeling the need to apologize, to explain himself. "You didn't need to wait up for me."

"I know that," she said, putting down her mending and going to the stove. "It's not that late – your ma and sister only went to bed half an hour ago. I just thought I'd make sure you got your supper."

She took a plate from the oven and set it down in front of him. It was full of stew, biscuits, and potatoes. His stomach rumbled at the sight of it.

"That's mighty kind of you, Miss Mayer."

"It's not really," she said, pouring him a cup of coffee. "It's just – well, today I got to thinking about how much I'm indebted to you for your help. You're there at the sheriff's office all day, slaving away to try and solve the mystery of Colin and the others like him...my mystery." She paused a moment, thinking things through. "It's not so important that it should take away your time with your family, not to mention your supper."

"It is so important," he corrected her gently, reaching out to arrest her with a hand around her wrist. She went utterly still at his touch, and he felt his heart beating in his throat. It wasn't a premeditated move, he hadn't intended to touch her, but – well, it was done now. He swallowed hard and continued. "It's important because it's your life that it's affected. Your entire future could be changed because of what some unknown man did – and you're not the only one."

"I know," she said softly. Her eyes were drawn downward, to where his hand was still clasped around her. "But my future is going to be changed no matter whether you find him or not. It's already done. After all – I'm here with you, aren't I?"

His mouth felt as dry as cotton. His heart was pounding into his head.

"Yes," he said, "you are."

The urge to draw her into his arms and kiss her was almost irresistible. The thought of it made him dizzy. But he couldn't – he wouldn't. She was a young woman who trusted in his protection, his gentlemanly instincts. With an effort, he released her and sat down.

To his surprise and gratification, she did not immediately run away to bed but sat down across from him, clearly continuing to seek out his company.

"How long have you been the sheriff, Tom?"

"About five years now," he said, picking up his fork. "I was a deputy for two years before that."

"Justice has been your life for a long time."

He nodded. "It has, at that."

She gave a quiet sigh.

"It's so frustrating, so sad, that people can behave so unjustly and simply…get away with it. They have no right to do so, and yet they escape punishment."

"I'll do everything I can to see that the man who took advantage of you and the others doesn't escape," he promised her. To his surprise, she shook her head.

"I wasn't thinking of that – for once. No, I was thinking of my father."

Her words seemed to invite questions, but the expression on her pretty face made it so clear she was lost in her own thoughts that he decided to hold his tongue and simply wait. He didn't have to wait for long; after a moment, without prompting or questions, she continued.

"He made some grave mistakes, my father did. I won't say he was a bad man, because I truly don't believe he was – but he was an imperfect man, as all men are. When my mother died, it broke his heart, and he stopped being truly good without ever being truly bad…I suppose he reaped what he sowed, in the end, as we are all warned."

Again, Tom felt the urge to ask a question, give her a prompt or a reaction, but she was not looking at him; her eyes were turned inward, and after another moment of silence she went on. "He got into debt – bad debt. I didn't understand just how badly things had gone. He never told me of what he owed, or to whom. But when I came home that day – the last day of his life – he was already close to dying. The man who he was in debt to killed him."

She pressed a hand to her stomach, and Tom winced. A bullet or a stab, she did not say, but the effect was the same and no less painful for not knowing. "I held his hand as he died…he apologized to me for what he had done, and I know that he wanted the best for me." She swallowed hard. "I promised him I would be taken care of."

Finally, her eyes met his again, and he saw she was waiting for him to speak.

"And you will be," he said. "That's a promise. Maybe not how you expected, maybe not by the man you thought – but taken care of, all the same."

"I haven't told anyone about this," she whispered. "I don't know why I'm burdening you with it."

Impulsively, he reached out and took her hand.

"A burden shared is a burden halved," he said. "I'm your friend, Miss Mayer, and I want to help you in any way I can."

She nodded, and the light shone in her blue eyes.

"Will there ever be real justice, Tom?" she asked him quietly. "For the other girls – for my father – for me?"

"If I have anything to say about it," Tom said, "yes. Yes, there will."

She squeezed his hand, smiling at him gratefully, and he felt again that surge of longing to draw her close to him. But she was on the other side of the table from him, and besides that, she was standing, ready to go to bed.

"Thank you, Tom."

"Thank you, Miss Mayer."

"Oh – and Tom…" She turned on the threshold. "I think, seeing as we're friends, you could call me Justine. If you'd like."

He couldn't help the wide smile that spread across his face.

"I'd like that very much, Justine."

"Good night."

"Good night."

For a long time after she left him, Tom Barnett sat in the comfortable silence of the kitchen, his uneaten plate of food growing cold in front of him, quietly contemplating just how much trouble he had gotten himself into when he allowed Justine Mayer to come and stay under his roof.

CHAPTER 6

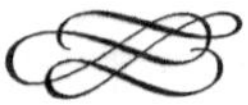

March rushed in on Fielder's Union with a dizzying array of springtime feeling. Though it was too early to write off the chance of more freezes and even snowfall, the cherry trees were already budding out into the epitome of aromatic bliss, with more delicate pink blossoms opening by the hour, it seemed. The almanac dourly predicted a late freeze, the farmers expressed doubts as to the wisdom of declaring it an early spring, but there was little argument as to the timeliness – and welcomeness – of the Ladies' Committee for the Organization of Community Events in Fielder's Union's presentation of the "End of Winter Ball."

"Are you quite sure I'm welcome to attend?" Justine asked Faith anxiously as the younger girl put up her hair for her.

"Of course, you are, why wouldn't you be?"

"Well, the dance is for the locals here in Fielder's Union, isn't it? And that doesn't exactly describe me."

"If you've lasted two weeks in Fielder's Union, you are a local," said Faith forthrightly. "Besides, I've just finished with your hair. You can't stay home now, not with a style as fine as that."

Justine smiled and glanced at herself in the mirror – and then took the time for a more thorough examination.

"Goodness, you've done a beautiful job, Faith. I could hardly recognize myself."

"The artist's skill is all in the materials," Faith said modestly, flexing her fingers. "If my hair was half as pretty as yours, I could hardly bear to put it up at all, to be honest. It looks so beautiful when you have it down, like waves of gold – but that's hardly the appropriate style for the dance." She brushed her hands together in a businesslike manner. "Now, on to your dress."

Justine had no dresses that were appropriate for a dance, either, but she had already expressed that concern and Faith had sailed over it just as blithely, refusing to let it be an obstacle to Justine's attendance at the dance.

As Faith rummaged through her wardrobe, Justine ventured, "I know that there are far more young men than women here in Fielder's Union…"

"Goodness, what an understatement. There are far more young men than women in the entirety of Arkansas, from what I can see."

"But won't the young women that are here in Fielder's Union resent the presence of an outsider – someone who might…" She shrugged. "Hone in on their undivided territory, so to speak?"

"Justine, you must stop grasping at straws. If you don't want to go to the dance, just say so." Faith turned to face her, a hand on her hip. Justine couldn't help but smile at her.

"I do want to go," she said. "And I suspect it's just as well, for if I did tell you I would rather stay home, you would make me go anyhow."

"You're not wrong," said Faith cheerily, turning back to the wardrobe.

"Do you suppose that – well – have you heard if – your brother is going to be in attendance?"

Faith had her head practically buried in the wardrobe, but Justine could hear her chuckle.

"He'd better be," she said, "or I'll drag him there myself. He ought to be waiting downstairs for us already, but I suppose we'll find out once we get you all kitted out." Finally, she stepped away from the wardrobe and turned to display her choice to Justine. "There. What do you think?"

Justine took a deep breath. The dress was far prettier than any she'd ever worn; her dresses tended to be rather drab, in tones of gray, brown, and black. This dress was a pattern of white flowers on a field of green, vibrant and youthful and positively the epitome of spring.

"For me? Are you sure?"

"Of course, I'm sure," said Faith, bringing it over to her. "And I think it will fit just about perfectly – it's a bit too long on me, so it will be ideal for you. Come on, Justine, I'll help you with it." She gave a happy sigh. "All the boys are just about going to fall over themselves when they see you walk into the room."

'All the boys' were not Justine's chief concern, but it was far from unpleasant to picture the reaction she might get. From Faith's earlier reckoning, there were some twenty-three young bachelors in Fielder's Union who were not attached to any woman, and there was only a small handful of young women who were similarly unattached. The sheer difference in numbers had been Faith's first argument for why Justine simply had to attend the dance.

Of course, catching the eye of twenty-three boys simultaneously was not Justine's plan; as a matter of fact, the more she thought about it, the more intimidating the prospect seemed.

On the other hand, if she could catch the eye of one young man in particular…say, the sheriff of Fielder's Union, for example…

She wondered, even as she contemplated her finished reflection in the mirror, whether it was even possible.

But the look on Tom's face as she came down the stairs answered it for her rather quickly.

He was waiting for them, as his younger sister had said he ought to be. And it was evident that he was, indeed, planning on attending the dance, though whether that was of his own accord or simply from a desire to avoid being dragged there by Faith was still in question. Justine's first thought, upon coming down the stairs and seeing him there, was of how glad she was that he was being so obedient to his sister's plans, and how handsome he was, all dressed up for the dance.

Her second thought, as their eyes met, was centered on the realization that Thomas Barnett clearly was thinking along the very same lines.

He opened his mouth as though he wanted desperately to speak, but nothing came out. He closed his mouth again, swallowed hard, gave a faint little grin of embarrassment, and tried once more.

"You look…"

She felt a blush coming on, even before the words were out of his mouth, and she was powerless to stop it. She dropped her eyes away from his gaze, and stepped toward him, taking the arm that he held out.

Tom shook his head and let out a long sigh.

"Beautiful," he said, so softly she could hardly hear it above the pounding of her heart.

CHAPTER 7

To his dying day, Tom Barnett suspected, he would never be sure whether he was grateful to Danny for insisting he take the afternoon off to attend the dance – or furious at him.

Oh, the dance was undoubtedly the event of the season. His mother and the Ladies' Committee had outdone themselves. The entire town hall was decked out within an inch of its life. There was plenty of pie to go around. Even the weather had thrown itself whole-heartedly into cooperating; he'd never seen so many cherry blossoms this early in the year.

And there was no question that the townsfolk of Fielder's Union were enjoying themselves thoroughly. From the moment he set foot inside the town hall, the walls were resounding with the sound of laughter, chatter, and the desperate attempts of a small string band trying to make itself heard over the happy din.

His presence did not go unnoticed, either. Though he had looked ahead with dread to being the only man his age without a wife and family of his own, the good people of Fielder's Union welcomed him to the party with overwhelming good cheer. He received so many thumps on the back he nearly staggered; his hand was appropriated for a handshake at every turn. Off to the side, he could see his little sister smiling smugly.

No, for all of that and more, he was grateful that Danny had offered to take over the office for the day so he could get away for a bit.

The main reason why he was holding back from being entirely thankful was standing at his side, her arm looped through his.

It wasn't that he resented going out in public with the prettiest woman in the room on his arm. It wasn't that he disliked Justine, or even that he was disinterested in her; quite the opposite. The biggest obstacle to his focus on his work, the biggest distraction he had ever yet encountered was Justine Mayer – and the more time he spent with her, the more of a distraction she became.

For that reason, and that reason alone, he couldn't help mentally giving Danny what-for, even as Justine tugged on his arm and drew him further into the room.

"Didn't they do a lovely job? It's the most beautiful thing I've ever seen."

"Yes," said Tom automatically, unable to take his eyes from her. "Beautiful…"

She met his glance swiftly and then looked away, blushing. Had she heard his murmur of that very same word when she had come down the stairs at the house? He wasn't sure. He hadn't intended for it to be heard; he hadn't intended for it to come out of his mouth at all. But every intention he held onto so tightly seemed to slip through his fingers when Justine was around.

In the two weeks she had been there in Fielder's Union, his zeal for the case of the mysterious letter writer had become more than simply a sheriff's interest in the cause of justice. It had become personal.

Whenever he found out who had been responsible for luring Justine here, he would arrest them – and then shake them by the hand and thank them when no one was watching.

The music started up again, louder this time. Someone must have given the band some encouragement. In response, the chatter of the crowd died away somewhat as half of the townsfolk chose their partners and arranged themselves for the first dance. Watching the orchestration of steps, Tom held his breath. He wanted to invite Justine to dance – of course he did. He wanted nothing more; he'd been dreaming of it for weeks.

But now that it came down to it – could he bring himself to ask?

Could he let himself dance with her, knowing all the while he was likely sealing his fate as his attachment and attraction to her grew and grew?

He caught a speculative glance from John Tanner, a young man close to Justine's age, who was currently partnerless and obviously itching to dance.

The doubt in his heart disappeared in an instant. Yes, he could. All of that and more. If he didn't dance with Justine, then what was the point of even being here?

He took her by the hand, and she turned to him. It would be foolish to try and make himself heard over the music, so he merely raised an eyebrow, giving her a questioning look. Her response was an eager smile, and with no words exchanged but complete understanding all the same, he led her onto the dance floor.

It was better than he had dreamed.

With the music directing them with every beat, the two of them moved in time with each other, perfectly matched. It was loud, a bit chaotic, breathless – and fun. Tom could hardly believe it. When was the last time he'd had fun?

When was the last time he'd allowed himself to think about anything other than his work?

And now his mind was full of nothing but Justine, Justine, Justine. As they moved through the steps, he caught glimpses of her pretty face, always smiling at him.

It could have been no more than a moment or more than an hour when the music stopped.

"Well, folks, looks like it's about time to take a little break," the band leader announced over the sound of clapping. "I reckon you all are getting pretty thirsty – well, that's nothing compared to the boys and me. See you over at the punch bowl, and perhaps we'd better settle just who is spiking it this time."

There was general laughter. Tom smiled ruefully and Justine chuckled.

"There's just something about Fielder's Union," she said. "It's like nowhere I've ever been before – or even heard of."

"The wild west, that's us," Tom agreed. "Next thing you know, there'll be bandits riding through town."

"Never," said Justine, smiling up at him adoringly. "Not with you as the sheriff, they wouldn't dare."

Tom glanced over at the crowd around the punch bowl. "Are you thirsty?"

"No, not really."

"Good."

He took her by the hand and pulled her after him toward the side door of the town hall.

It was cool outside, bordering on cold, but not nearly as frigid as it should still by rights have been in early March. The nighttime had settled down over the town like a velvet blanket, and the moon had just risen.

"Must be just about seven o'clock."

"Is it that late already?" At his side, Justine shook her head and smiled. "It's hard to believe – it seems that we've only just arrived."

"Time flies when you're having fun."

Her eyes met his.

"Are you?" she asked. "Having fun, I mean."

"Justine, I'm enjoying this evening more than I've ever enjoyed anything in my entire life. And do you know why?"

She tilted her head, looking up at him coyly through her lashes. "I'd like you to tell me."

He slipped a hand onto her cheek and leaned down. "You," he whispered.

Of all the times he had felt the urge to kiss her, it had never been quite so strong as it was in this moment. Scarcely had he brushed her lips with his own when he felt a shock go through the two of them – almost immediately followed by a *crack*, and the sound of far-off thunder.

He lifted his head, instantly on the alert.

"Lightning?" Justine asked, turning her eyes heavenward.

"Gunfire," said Thomas grimly.

CHAPTER 8

Thomas Barnett was a big believer in overreacting. Even if only to avoid under-reacting, it seemed worth the energy and effort. He felt that it was a big part of what made him a successful sheriff.

It wasn't that the sound of gunshots was unusual in Fielder's Union. What was unusual was the timing – with practically the entire town in the town hall behind him, what was there to get in a shootout about?

And then there was the other noise, the sound of thunder that was far away – but rapidly getting closer.

They were around the corner from the main thoroughfare that ran through Fielder's Union, on which the inn, café, and sheriff's station all fronted. The thunderous noise was coming from the east, and it was worrisomely familiar. Tom raced around the corner and caught himself before stepping into the street. Justine nearly ran into him, and he threw both arms around her, pulling her back against him.

"Stampede!" he shouted against the din, which had suddenly grown immensely louder.

It was cattle. Longhorn cattle, freed from their pens and whipped into a panic by the gunshots behind them. They came ripping and roaring down the street, tumbling into pillars and knocking down awnings, smashing the glass of some shop windows as they passed haphazardly.

Tom turned his head to look down the street. There were few people around at this time of night, but a handful of them were in front of the town hall, taking a breath of the fresh night air.

"Get inside," he yelled at them, waving an arm. "Get back inside now."

Amid the sound of fright and scurrying, he turned back to see the cattle rushing ever closer. At the back of the terrified herd, he could just barely make out the larger shapes of men on horseback, calling and whooping and still occasionally shooting off a pistol to ensure that the cattle continued on their disastrous rampage. But the men were not following the cattle, and the darkness with the early moon was too thick to make out any features. Tom ducked back toward the side door, Justine hurrying along at his side. His arm was still around her.

He stopped just inside the door and scanned the crowd, which was murmuring over the noise of destruction from outside.

"Everyone just stay put," he called out. Only those nearest could hear, but he saw several of them nod and begin to spread the word. He turned to Justine and put a hand on each shoulder.

"Justine, I know you're frightened – but everything is going to be all right." His eyes met hers and searched; yes, there was fear there, but there was also trust, and it made his heart warm and glow. He pulled her toward him swiftly and kissed her. It was not the kiss he had been waiting for, but he was sure that if he put it off, he would only live to regret it. Who knew what the night might bring?

"Go and find Faith and Ma," he instructed her. "Then come back and stay right here until I return for you."

"Tom, where are you going?"

The fear in her voice was not fear for herself, he knew. It was fear for him. He traced his fingertips down her cheek.

"I'm the sheriff," he reminded her gently. "Wherever there's trouble, that's where I belong."

It was almost impossible to tear himself away from her side, but he managed it by holding his breath and going out at a run.

The cattle stampede had more or less spent itself in the past few minutes, and they were dispersed all over the main street and some of the side streets, lowing and stamping and breathing heavily. In the cold night air, the heat from their bodies rose as a fine fog. Tom ran past them and headed for the sheriff station.

To his horror, the door was standing open, the room inside empty – and there was something dark on the floor.

"Danny?"

It was pointless to call, but he felt he had to anyhow. The fire had died out; no one had been here for some time, it seemed. He bent over the dark spots and touched a fingertip to them; it came away red. Sure enough, the spots were blood, quite fresh.

Was Danny hurt? Where was he? What had happened?

And what on earth did the intentional cattle stampede have to do with it?

No one was hurt in the stampede, but that was just a matter of happenstance, wasn't it? If it had been a usual evening, there was every chance that people would have been hurt, maybe even killed. The cattle ran faster than some grown men and women, and much faster than most children—inexorably bearing down on everything in their path – the thought made him shudder.

Was it just a happy accident that it had happened during the dance? Or was it planned, deliberate – more an act of terrorizing the town than of intention to cause harm?

His mind was a whirl of disjointed thoughts and unanswered questions. He was less alert than he should have been as he stepped back out of the sheriff's office and headed to the west, toward Danny's house on the other side of town. At his side, he wore his pistol; in his left hand, he carried his rifle. Whatever happened, he wanted to be ready…

As he passed the first alleyway to the west past the sheriff's station, an arm reached out of the darkness and grabbed him, pulling him in out of the light of the moon.

Tom gave a shout, the pistol leaping into his hand. But there was just enough light to see the features of the man who had accosted him, and he froze, shock washing over him at his own recognition.

The older man chuckled dryly, nodding. "Good to see you again, Tom."

Tom swallowed hard, trying to wrap his mind around the series of surprises that had made up the majority of his evening. In return, he nodded back.

"You too, Marshal Melson."

CHAPTER 9

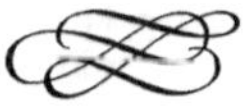

"Eliza? Faith?"

"Oh, Justine," Faith flung herself into Justine's arms, practically weeping with worry. "I'm so glad you're all right. When we heard the gun shots, and then someone said there were cattle stampeding, and I couldn't find you anywhere…"

"I know, I know. I'm sorry." Justine smoothed a hand over her young friend's tousled hair, reaching her other hand out to take Eliza's arm. The older woman's face was drawn tight with worry, and Justine tried to soothe her with her touch. "I was with Tom – we had stepped outside when we heard the noise."

"Did you see the cattle? Oh, it must have been terrifying."

"He kept me well away. I was never in any danger – and neither was he," Justine assured them.

Faith raised her head and looked around, obviously searching for her brother.

"Where is he? Where is Tom?"

"If I know my son," said Eliza heavily, "he's wherever the heart of the trouble is." She put an arm around her daughter and drew her close. "He's the sheriff, Faith – he's got a job to do. Protect the town, keep the peace, pursue justice."

"Justice, sure, but not a cattle stampede."

"Someone deliberately caused it," Justine said. "It was no accident – there were men on horseback behind the herd. I couldn't see them very well, but I heard them." She shivered. "I think they were enjoying the fright and destruction they caused."

"Some men are like that, I'm afraid," said Eliza. "And those are the men Thomas wants to stop." She shook her head. "I've no doubt that he's on the trail."

"I wish I knew where he was," Justine admitted, twisting her fingers together abstractedly. "I know he's the sheriff, and he's a brave man who can't shirk his duty – but I still wish he was here by us, and safe."

"Of course, you do, my dear," Eliza said, putting her other arm around Justine and drawing her closer just as she had done with her daughter. "You care about my son – I know you do – and that's to your credit, for he's a good man who deserves to be cared about. But for now, we must wait."

"Yes." Justine bit her lip. "He said we should stay here in the town hall. He wants to keep us safe, even if he can't be here with us."

"Just like him," said Eliza, closing her eyes and sighing.

The three of them stood huddled together for some time, while around them the townsfolk of Fielder's Point argued and discussed what should be done. Several of the men headed out, despite the sheriff's warning, to try and find the culprits behind the cattle stampede, or at least identify who the cattle belonged to. More dispersed to examine and assess the damage that had been done. Soon, there were only older men, women, and children left in the town hall, most in small groups speaking in low tones, waiting for their menfolk to return and take them home to safety.

But the first man to come into the town hall was not returning, for he had not been there to begin with. As he entered the hall and stood looking around him, Justine was shocked to recognize Danny Turner, his face twisted into a pensive expression that bordered on the tormented. As he caught sight of them, the expression cleared up and he strode toward them through the crowd.

"There you are, finally. Thought I was going to have to wade through each and every group of little hens in here to find you three."

"Danny?" said Eliza, frowning. "Why aren't you with Tom? I'm sure he's in greater need of you than we are."

Danny paused and turned his attention to Eliza. The look he gave her was inscrutable, impossible to read clearly – but something about it gave Justine a chill all the way to her bones.

"What is it, Deputy Turner?" she asked, anxious for him to look away from Eliza.

"As a matter of fact," said Danny, "Tommy sent me to find you three and bring you out to safety."

Eliza and Faith turned to look at Justine, who hesitated.

"But Tom – Sheriff Barnett told us to stay here until he came for us himself."

"Did he?" Danny raised an eyebrow. "Is that precisely, exactly what he said?"

"I – I think so. I suppose I can't remember exactly word for word…"

"Well, what I'm sure he *meant* was to wait until he sent word that it was safe," Danny drawled, emphasizing every other word. "Whether he intended to come for you himself or not is beside the point, because here I am." He gestured to himself. "I'm the word that he sent, to tell you it's safe to come with me – or it will be, if you do as you're told."

"Danny," said Faith, quietly, "what happened to your hand?"

His hand, Justine now saw, was poorly wrapped in a strip of fabric that had once been white but was now dirty. There was blood seeping through it. He lifted the hand and waved it at them with a wry chuckle.

"Spotted that, did you, little sister? Well, this ought to convince you if nothing else does. I've been fighting with the enemy while you three are huddling in here with the rest of the henhouse – fighting with the enemy long before Sheriff Tommy showed up, as a matter of fact. Now, if this doesn't tell you that I'm a trustworthy and honest fellow, worthy of being listened to – I don't know what will."

Again, Faith and Eliza looked to Justine, who swallowed hard past the lump in her throat. There was something undeniably wrong with Danny's behavior – and his claim that the wound in his hand was proof that he fought on the side of justice could be entirely false. Who knew where that cut had come from?

But at the same time, she had no real reason to doubt his word. After all, suppose Tom had intended to come for them when he'd told her to wait, but things had changed between now and then. There was no doubt that something dangerous, something important was happening in the town. Tom couldn't know all circumstances ahead of time –

And she wanted, rather desperately, to believe that he had, in fact, sent Danny to collect them. She wanted to believe anything that would bring her back to Tom's side.

With another second of hesitation, she nodded.

Danny's demeanor changed almost immediately. The smile that spread over his face was positively benevolent, kind, angelic.

He reached out to her with one hand, inviting her to take his. The upturned palm with its bloodied bandage was certainly not appealing, but his smile turned insistent, and at last she reached out to touch her fingertips to his, accepting his help to be led out of the town hall.

Walking alongside her toward the door, Danny gave a deep, throaty chuckle.

"Almost done now, Miss Justine," he said. "I promise you this – it's nearly over at last."

CHAPTER 10

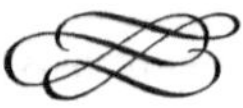

Tom leaned his rifle against the wall and folded his arms, staring at the unexpected face in front of him.

"What are you doing here? I thought you were still stationed in Lampoc."

"I was," Marshal Adrian Melson said slowly, "until I got wind of what was happening over here in Fielder's Union."

"What do you mean?"

The older man, who had a grizzled beard and a hawklike nose, raised a thick and equally grizzled eyebrow at him.

"Don't you ever read your mail, boy?"

"If you mean the letter that you wrote, it got lost in the shuffle somehow before I had a chance," Tom admitted. "It's my own fault, but in my defense, I was rather distracted – well, I told you all this in the letter."

Now it was Melson's turn to look quizzically at him. "What letter?"

"What letter? My letter – the letter I wrote you after I misplaced yours. I sent it to you last week."

Melson shook his head. "Never received any letter."

"But – it must have gotten there by now." Tom chewed on his lower lip. "How on earth…"

"You posted it yourself? With your own hands?"

"Well, no, Danny took it for me. He offered…"

"Deputy Turner?" Melson put his head back against the wall behind him and groaned. "There's your answer, then, Tom. Do you know what my letter to you, the one you so carelessly misplaced, contained?"

"What?"

"A stark warning to look out for your deputy, as I'd had reports that suggested he might be in over his head with the Hound Gang."

Tom's eyebrows shot upward. "The Hound Gang?"

Melson nodded. "The very same. Now, I suspect that part of the reason my letter was 'misplaced,' as you say, was a deliberate act on the part of Deputy Turner – after all, you may be a bit rash sometimes, young man, but you're not what anyone would call disorganized. And if you allowed him to take out your letter to the post, well, then – nothing easier than disposing of it in the same way. I reckon he's been behind any other difficulties you've had with sending and receiving communication, too."

Tom put his hand to his forehead.

"I can't believe it," he muttered. "Danny – I've known him for years…"

"Believe it," Melson advised him frankly. "If you want more proof…"

He pulled aside his jacket, and Tom couldn't stop the exclamation that leapt to his lips.

"You're bleeding."

"I know it," Melson said, letting his jacket fall back into place with a slight grunt of pain. "Knew it when it first started, too, and let me tell you, I won't let that young pup escape just for this, let alone everything else he's done. I went looking for you in the sheriff's office and surprised him picking the lock on your desk drawer – going after the petty cash, I imagine."

He grinned. "Startled him pretty good, I reckon, for he cut himself with his own lock pick. But he pulled a pistol on me before I could do much else and shot me in the side." He put a hand tenderly over the area where he had bandaged himself up. "He's not too good a shot, is he, your deputy?"

"No," said Tom grimly. "He's not. But good enough to hit you, evidently."

"Winged me," said Melson dismissively. "I'll be fine, and it won't take me off the case. Did knock me down for a bit, but that's all – when I came to, he had scarpered and there were cattle roaming the streets." He eyed Tom. "I suppose you'd like an explanation for that, too."

Tom sighed. He had never felt at such a loss in his life; and after all his thoughts about performing as a good sheriff, too.

"If it's not too much trouble."

"Well, here's the long and short of it. You and me have been talking about those mysterious letters that keep luring young women here under false pretenses, and I've been keeping an ear to the ground from Lampoc. Haven't heard much about that letter business, but I did start hearing rumblings about sightings of the Hound Gang. Now, Gerry Troy runs the gang ever since his pa died, and he's been ever so slowly inching closer to Fielder's Union over the past year. Last place they hit was a bank just south of Lampoc, two months ago. Been dead quiet ever since then – until I get a tip that your deputy is dirty when he ought to be clean."

"The stampede…"

"Fostering fear among the townsfolk," Melson said promptly. "That's how the Hound Gang operates. They terrorized a town north of here for months until the townspeople raided the bank themselves, handed over a king's ransom just to be able to stop worrying about their children's safety when they were out playing in the street. Never heard of a gang before that got innocent folks to do their dirty work for them, but that's the hallmark of the Hound Gang."

"And this is how they're starting?" Tom shook his head. "I can't believe it…"

"I rode into town last night, decided to keep an eye out before I made myself known. Well, the cat's out of the bag now, but at least we can fight them together."

"What kind of lawman lets a gang try to take over his town without even realizing it?" Tom lamented.

But Melson clapped him on the shoulder heartily.

"A lawman that expects his deputy to be as decent and upright as he is," he said. "Your only mistake was in trusting too much, Tom – and that's something that only experience can teach you, I'm afraid."

"What do we do?"

"My men are on their way. If we go out against the gang now, they'll disappear, evaporate – the only way is to bide our time, let them think they've won the first round."

Tom clenched his jaw. "That's easier said than done."

"It is, right enough," Melson agreed affably. "But that's another thing that experience will have to teach you, Tom."

"What's that?"

"Patience. Patience, and the art of keeping your mouth shut."

Tom glanced toward the mouth of the back street, taking in a deep breath. Suddenly, he went very still.

"What about when there's hostages involved?" he asked quietly. "What do you do then?"

Melson followed his gaze to the sight of Danny Turner, cheerfully leading three women down the street toward the west.

"Your family?"

Tom nodded. His throat was dry, his eyes fixed on the worried, dear, familiar faces of his mother, his sister, and the woman he loved.

"My family," he whispered hoarsely. "Adrian, I can't just let him…"

Melson hesitated, calculating the actions that should be taken. Finally, he nodded.

"Go on, then," he said. "But remember, my men are on the way…"

Tom nodded. Swallowing hard, he left the marshal behind and stepped out, alone, into the empty street.

CHAPTER 11

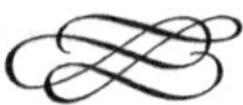

It took all the self-control that Tom Barnett possessed to keep himself from rushing across the road, stomping his erstwhile deputy to the ground, and pulling the women in his life away from the young man's greedy, contemptible hands. Somehow, though, he managed it, walking calmly across the street in their direction, and only calling out once he was much closer.

"Danny. Girls."

They turned as one. Even in the misleading light of the moon, he could see the fear glinting in the eyes of the three women.

Danny, on the other hand, bore an expression that could only be described as poorly-hidden fury masked thinly by rapt concern.

"Tommy. There you are. I've been looking for you everywhere."

"I went looking for you, too." He continued to walk toward them, hands at his sides, though his palms were fairly itching to reach for his pistol. "Guess we missed each other in all the ruckus – glad you didn't get run over by a bull."

This, of course, was a blatant lie; he would have liked nothing better.

Danny blinked at him innocently.

"Guess you heard all of that. I wasn't in town – I'd heard gunshots earlier and headed out to look for the source."

"Did you? I didn't hear any gunshots until the cattle were already stampeding."

"Huh. Guess you must have been…distracted." Danny slid an arm through Justine's, pulling her closer to him. His smile took on a knife's edge, sharp and dangerous. "How did the dancing go, anyhow? I meant to ask – anyone get swept off their feet?"

"Let go of me," Justine said.

"You look faint, Miss Justine. I don't want you to fall – I'm being a gentleman."

She pulled her arm away from his and stepped clear of him. Her face was tight with stress, but her eyes were fixed on Tom.

Danny shook his head and swore a little under his breath.

"Guess we'd better stop play-acting," he said, and in the next moment he had reached out for Justine, wrapping one arm around her shoulders, and bringing her tucked in close and tight to his chest. In the same motion, he pulled his pistol from its holster and held it with the muzzle pointed at the side of her head.

Faith screamed and Eliza pulled her daughter toward her, backing up away from Danny so quickly that the two of them nearly stumbled and went down in the middle of the road. Justine made not a single sound; her throat was taut, but she would not scream.

Her eyes were fixed on Tom.

"Now," said Danny, "what I want you to do, Sheriff Tommy, is to take your pistol out of the holster and put it on the ground. Very gently, mind. We don't want any accidental discharge."

Tom hesitated, and Danny arched an eyebrow at him.

"We all know you think you're a hero," he said. "And we all know what a fantastic marksman you are – don't think I'm going to allow room for you to show off to impress your girl, here." The mouth of the pistol drifted closer to Justine's temple. "Every second you stall is a second she draws closer to death."

"All right, all right." Tom did as he was told, setting the pistol down gently and backing away from it a few steps. Arms at his side, he stared at Danny. "I don't understand. Why are you doing this?"

"Why does anyone do anything, Tommy? Fame and fortune."

There was no use in hiding what he knew; Danny obviously had guessed he'd talked with the marshal.

"The Hound Gang," he said slowly. "What have you got to do with them?"

Danny shook his head and laughed.

"Everything and nothing," he said. "I'm just sitting pretty to inherit the empire of crime, that's all. My uncle runs the gang – and he's got big plans for Fielder's Union. Move in, take over." He nodded in satisfaction. "He's about ready to retire, and figures this'll be the place to do it."

"Why?"

"Well, family connections, for one," Danny said with a smirk. "And he happens to know there's a sheriff who will turn a blind eye to anything he chooses to do."

"I'll never…"

"Not you, you fool," Danny snapped at him. "Me. What would we keep you around for? You're worse than useless." He turned his head to look at Justine. "How can you stand him, Miss Justine? Don't you just want to slap him every time he opens his mouth?"

"Don't you touch him," said Justine, voice low but strong.

Danny laughed again.

"Listen to her. They do build them tough in Boston – I knew that was the right place to cull from."

Tom blinked at him.

"What are you talking about?"

"Oh, don't tell me that you didn't put two and two together?" Danny rolled his eyes. "And you've been sheriff for how long? Can't even figure out what's right under his nose."

"You've been writing the letters?" Tom said slowly. "Bringing the girls here...but why?"

"Like I said," Danny reminded him. "Big plans. The Hound Gang wants to settle here in Fielder's Union – properly settle. A few women to pick from could make all the difference to the happiness of my uncle's men – didn't really matter how they were brought here." He shrugged. "It was my own idea, and I don't hesitate to say it worked perfectly." He grinned again at Justine. "Think I might keep this one for myself, though."

"But the girls – they had nothing when they came here for a lie. Most of them are working upstairs at the saloon…"

"What do we care?" Danny said callously. "We want to pick and choose – whether we choose a wife, a mistress, or an hour now and then, it's all the same to us." He shook his head, then turned once more to Justine. "You know, he really is a fool…"

Justine raised her leg and stomped down hard, putting all her weight into it, right on Danny's foot. At the same time she dropped her weight, slithering down through his arm and away from his grasp. Tom rushed forward as the other man yowled in pain, getting in a solid hit to Danny's face before his deputy came roaring back. The two got into a mutual grip, each trying to take down the other, but they were of similar weight, size, and strength, and it was impossible to tell what way things would fall.

Tom heard a woman's sob, and cast a swift glance to the side, just to ensure that his family was all safe. Justine had crawled over to where Eliza and Faith sat huddled together – they were safe, but the brief second cost him. Danny overpowered him, knocked him sideways with a punch to the gut, and then back again with one to the other side. Tom bent double, his breath escaping him in a wheeze, and Danny doubled his fists together to bring down on the back of his neck.

The sound of a shot froze them all in a tableau.

Then Tom fell backward.

Then, for the first time, there was a cry from Justine. She stood up, her golden hair loose about her shoulders, her blue eyes wide, her face full of a terrible fear – and a terrible anger.

But it was Danny who had been hit. Though he was still standing, his face dazed and confused, when he reached up to the wound in his stomach, his hand came away covered in blood.

He slumped to his knees soundlessly.

Justine was at Tom's side, hands sliding over his limbs, his chest, checking frantically for any wounds. He smiled up at her dizzily.

"I like your hair like that…"

"Oh, for goodness's sake, Thomas Barnett."

He sat up just enough to pull her down within kissing range, and at last gave her the kiss he had been waiting for. They sat together, close and tight, for a moment before he let her go, smoothing a hand over her cheek.

She helped him to stand, and he turned to face the stalwart figure of Marshal Melson, who was slowly walking up to them from his previous hiding place in the alleyway. He carried a smoking rifle – Tom's rifle.

"Reckon I don't have as good an aim as you do, boy," said Melson. "But it turned out all right in the end."

Tom breathed a sigh of relief.

"Thought you were waiting for your men," he said.

Melson grinned at him. "Like I said, patience is a lesson that needs to be learned by any good lawman," he said, and tucked the rifle under his arm. "Guess I'd better get on back to school."

Tom shook his head and put his arm around Justine. He held his other arm out toward his mother and sister, who came to join the family huddle, crying tears of joy and relief.

"What about the gang?" Justine said. "And the Marshal's men? Will everything be all right?"

Tom smiled down at her and pulled her a little tighter. "If I have anything to say about it," he said, "everyone's going to get just what they deserve."

The End

CONTINUE READING...

Thank you for reading **Rescuing the Duped Bride!** Are you wondering **what to read next?** Why not read *The Bride's Rancher?* **Here's a peek for you:**

The last dying rays of the sun cast long shadows ahead of her as she trod wearily through the dusty town. Winter wasn't far off, yet the warm days of rural Pennsylvania continued for the time being. Fire and lamplight illuminated the windows of the cottage, a sight that never ceased to bring peace to her mind and soul.

Chickens still pecked in the small yard as Elaine opened the gate in the fence, then climbed the few steps to the front porch. Juggling the sack she held, she turned the brass handle to open the door. The warm odors of stew cooking on the stove greeted her, as did the sight of her mother seated near the hearth.

"Mama," Elaine said cheerfully. "I've brought bread. It's a couple of days old, but Mrs. Henderson gave it to me."

Her mother, Leah Rockmont, merely nodded without smiling. "That was nice of her."

Leah seldom smiled these days, thus Elaine wasn't surprised at her lack of enthusiasm. "She also gave me a few apples she can't sell, and potatoes."

"She is a kind woman."

Taking her prizes to the kitchen at the rear of the cottage, Elaine set the sack on the table. Under the curious gaze of her young niece, Elizabeth, she placed the long loaf of stale bread, the bruised apples and potatoes growing eyes on the counter. "Fish stew? Where'd the fish come from?"

"I caught it," Elizabeth replied. "In the brook."

"It smells delicious."

A quiet child, Elizabeth came to live with Elaine and Leah the year before. Elaine's older brother and his wife were killed when their house caught fire. Elizabeth only survived because her father succeeded in throwing her out a second story window before succumbing to the smoke and flames. Elizabeth rolled across the porch roof before tumbling into a patch of shrub, and escaped death with only a few scratches and bruises.

Like Leah, she never laughed, and her smiles came infrequently.

"We'll have a feast tonight," Elaine went on, taking bowls and plates from the cupboard to set the table.

Visit HERE To Read More!

https://ticahousepublishing.com/mail-order-brides.html

THANKS FOR READING!

If you **love Mail Order Bride Romance**, <u>Visit Here</u>

https://wesrom.subscribemenow.com/

to find out about all **<u>New Susannah Calloway Romance</u> <u>Releases!</u> We will let you know as soon as they become available!**

If you enjoyed *Rescuing the Duped Bride*, would you kindly take a couple minutes to leave a positive review on Amazon? It only takes a moment, and positive reviews truly make a difference. Thank you so much! I appreciate it!

Turn the page to discover more Mail Order Bride Romances just for you!

MORE MAIL ORDER BRIDE ROMANCES FOR YOU!

We love clean, sweet, adventurous Mail Order Bride Romances and have a lovely library of Susannah Calloway titles just for you!

Box Sets — A Wonderful Bargain for You!

https://ticahousepublishing.com/bargains-mob-box-sets.html

Or enjoy Susannah's single titles. You're sure to find many favorites! (Remember all of them can be downloaded FREE with Kindle Unlimited!)

Sweet Mail Order Bride Romances!

https://ticahousepublishing.com/mail-order-brides.html

ABOUT THE AUTHOR

Susannah has always been intrigued with the Western movement - prairie days, mail-order brides, the gold rush, frontier life! As a writer, she's excited to combine her love of story with her love of all that is Western. Presently, Susannah lives in Wyoming with her hubby and their three amazing children.

www.ticahousepublishing.com
contact@ticahousepublishing.com